BY MARGARET MERRIFIELD M.D.
ILLUSTRATED BY HEATHER COLLINS

**AN EDUCATIONAL STORYBOOK FOR CHILDREN AND THEIR CAREGIVERS
ABOUT HIV/AIDS AND SAYING GOODBYE**

Stoddart

Published in 1995 by
Stoddart Publishing Co. Limited
34 Lesmill Road
Toronto, Ontario
Canada M3B 2T6
(416) 445-3333

Canadian Cataloguing in Publication Data

Merrifield, Margaret.
    Soon will come the morning light

ISBN 0-7737-5704-X

1. AIDS (Disease) — Juvenile fiction.   I. Collins, Heather.
II. Title.

PS8576.E77S6 1995   jC813'.54   C94-931956-2
PZ7.M47So 1995

Stoddart Publishing gratefully acknowledges the support
of the Canada Council, Ontario Ministry of Culture and
Communications, Ontario Arts Council, and Ontario
Publishing Centre in the development of writing and
publishing in Canada.

Special acknowledgements to my husband, Keith and the readers
                                                        — M.M.

Printed in Hong Kong

For my mother, who loved me her entire life

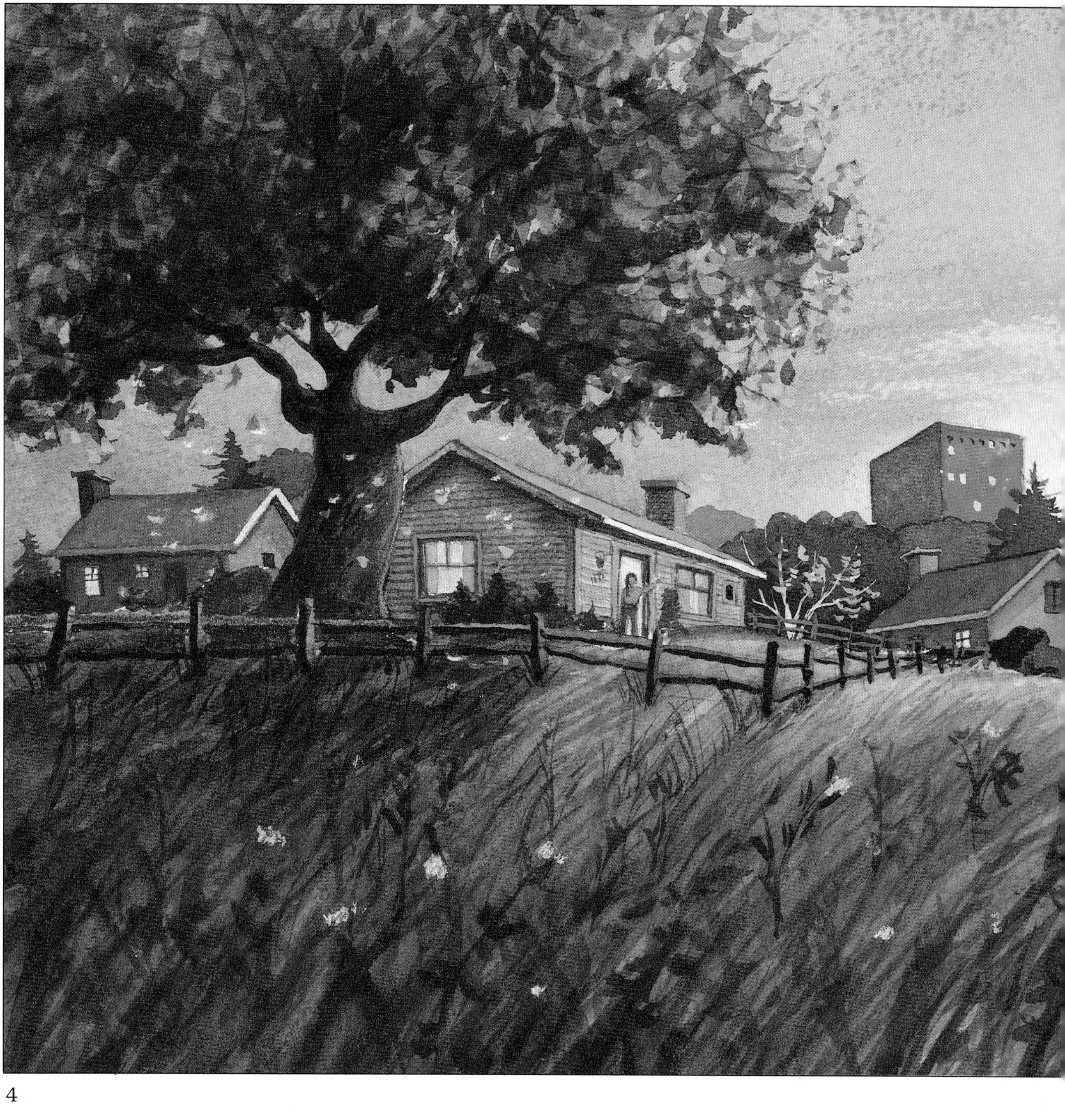

"Time to come in," Mother called to Max and Maggie. "It's getting dark."

Maggie raced Max to the door. "I won," she shouted. "I got here first."

"You always have to be first," said Max.

"Well, I'm older."

"Only by fifteen minutes," teased Max. "Besides, I'm smarter. I learned to tie my shoelaces before you did."

"Only by fifteen minutes."

"Time for bed," Mother said.

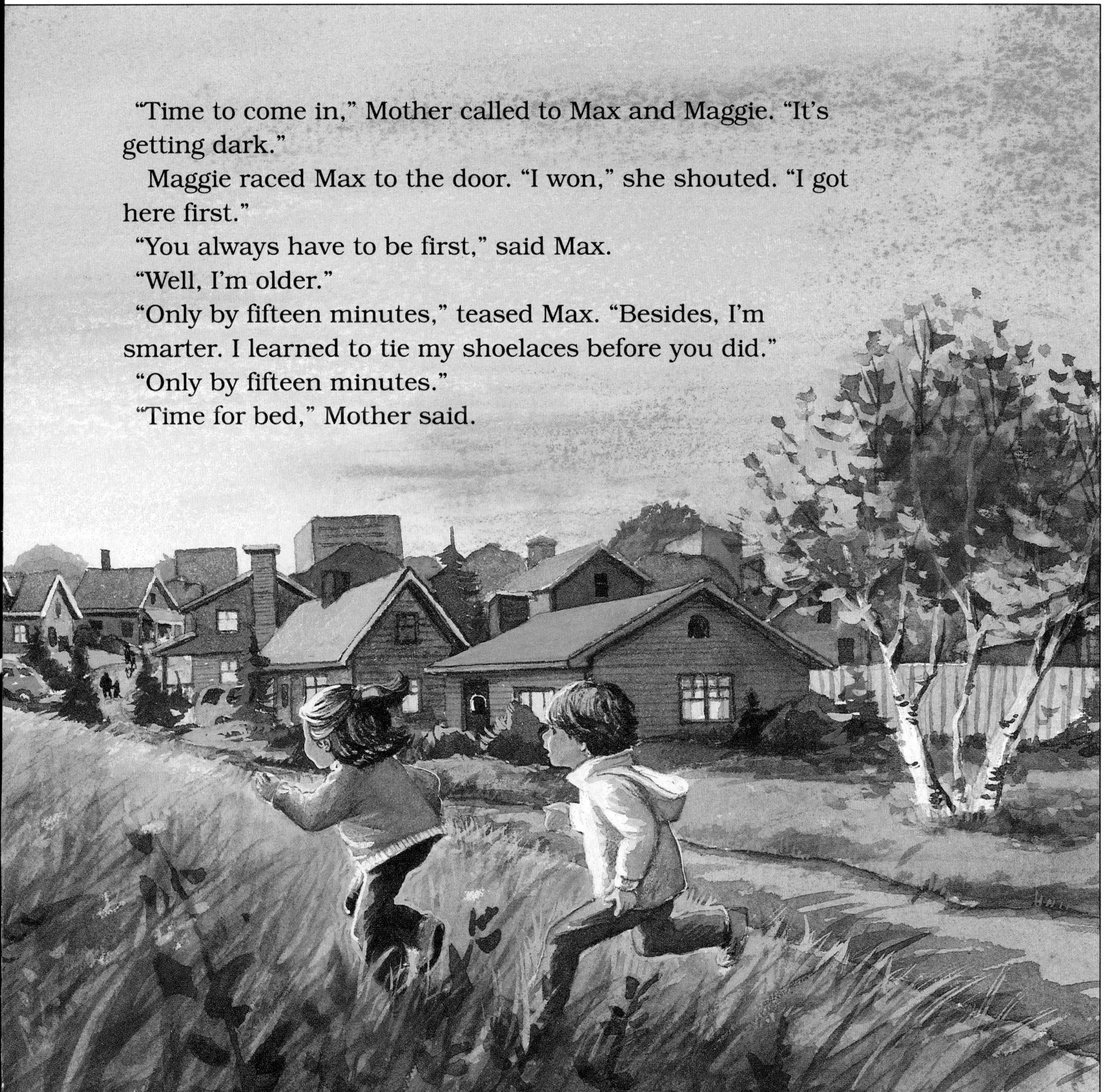

Almost every night since Max and Maggie were born, their mother sang this song to them:

In the sky, a twinkling light,
Good night, star bright.
Soon will come the morning light,
Good night, sleep tight.

Then she whispered, "Dream a sweet dream tonight."

It was a wonderful way to fall asleep.

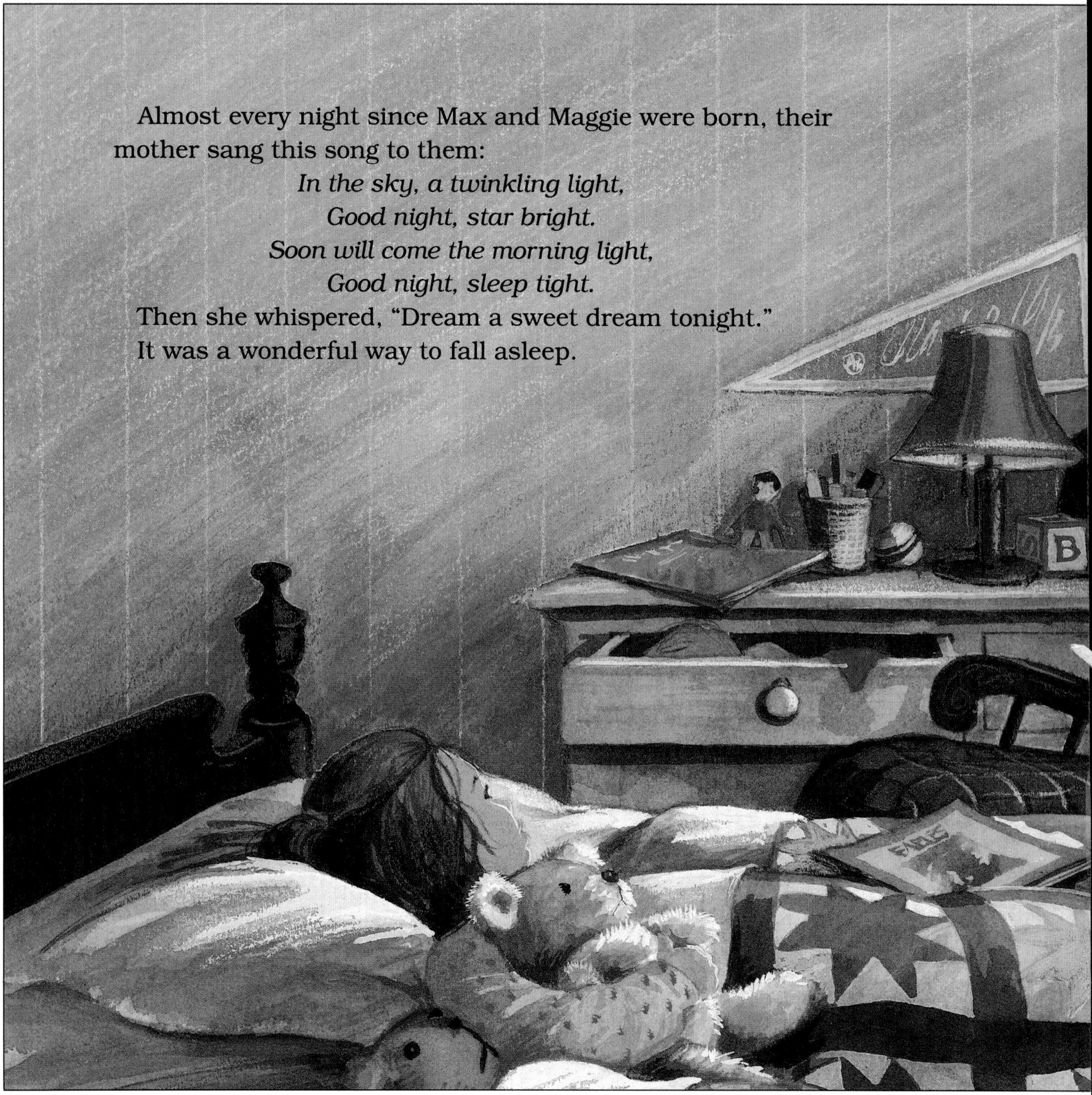

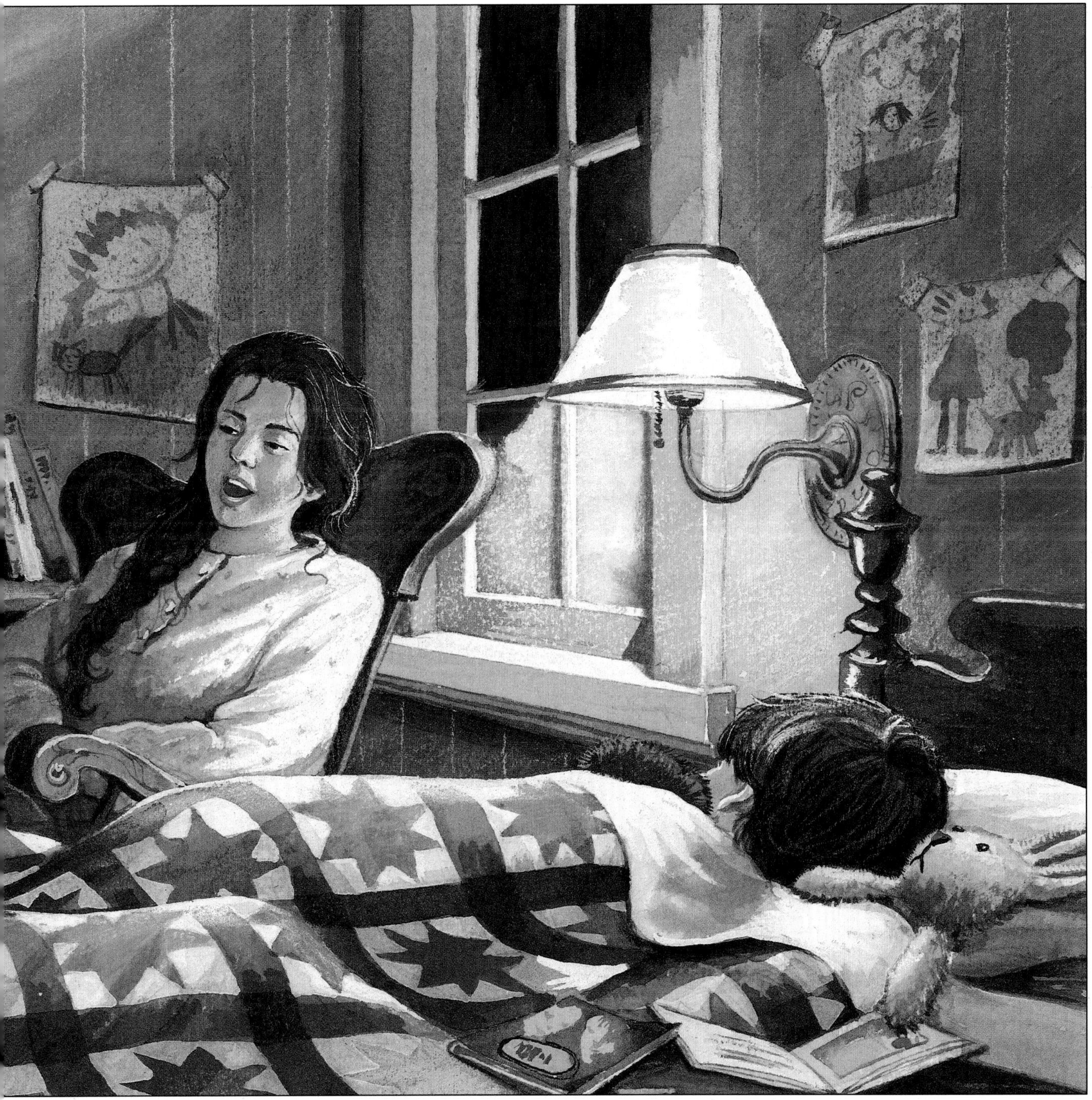

The next morning Max said, "I don't want to go to school. My throat hurts, and I'm hot."

Maggie was scared. "Will Max get sicker and stay in the hospital like you do?" she asked her mother.

"No," answered Mother. "He'll be better in a few days." And he was.

But by the time Maggie had worn out her running shoes and Max needed a haircut, Mother was very sick. Unlike Max, she did not get better in a few days.

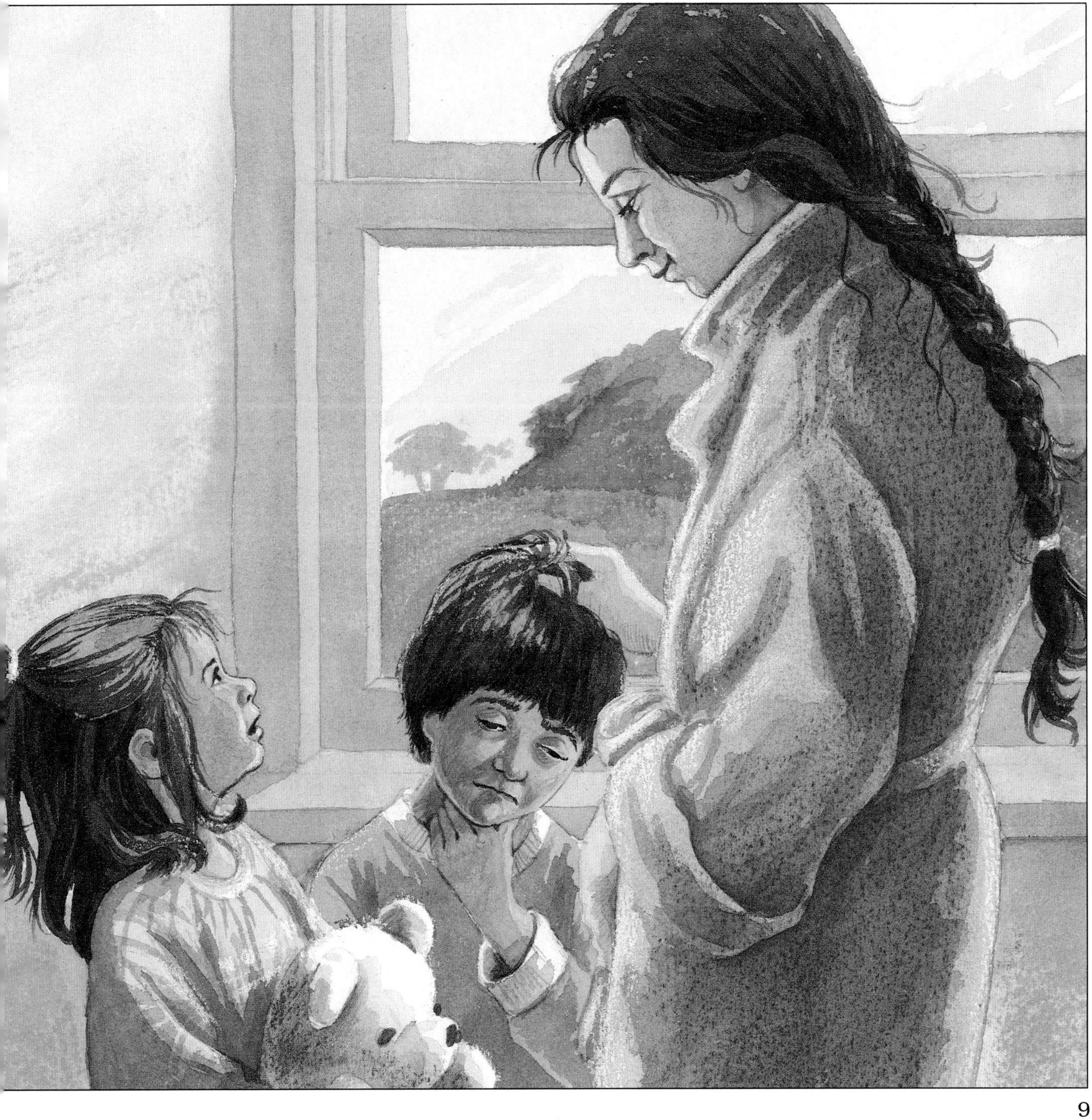

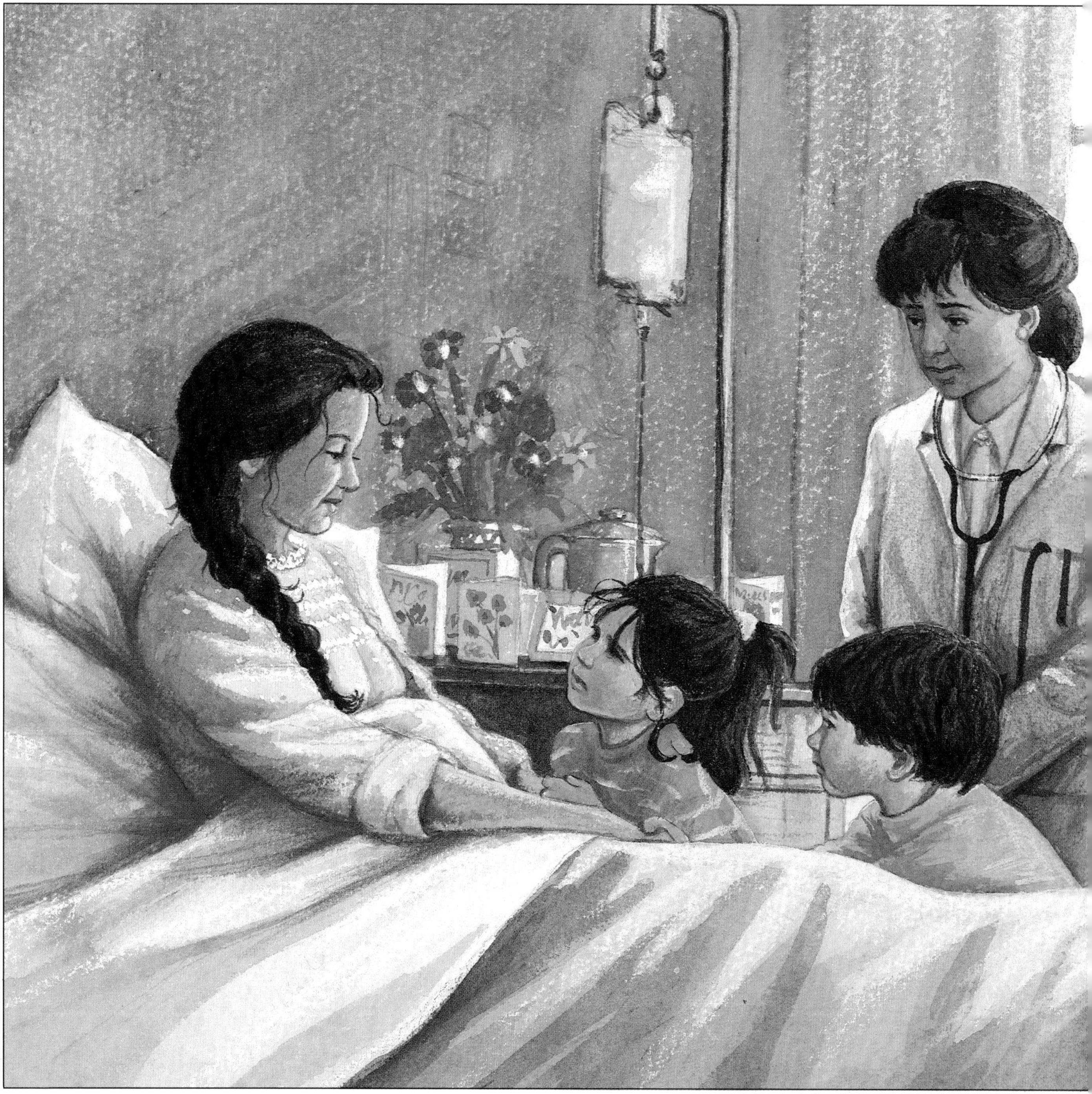

She had to go to the hospital. Uncle Dan and Auntie Beth came to take care of the twins.

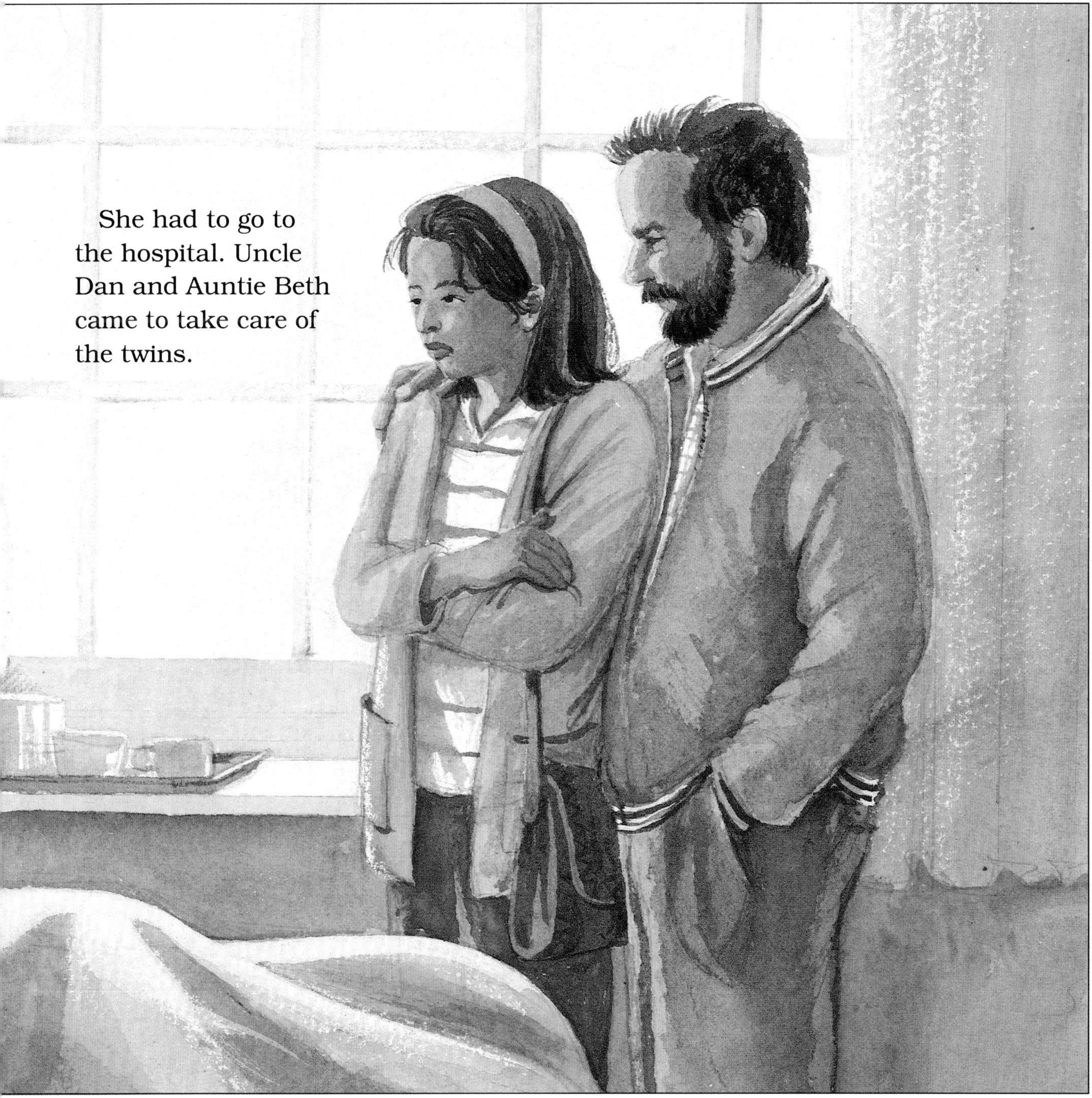

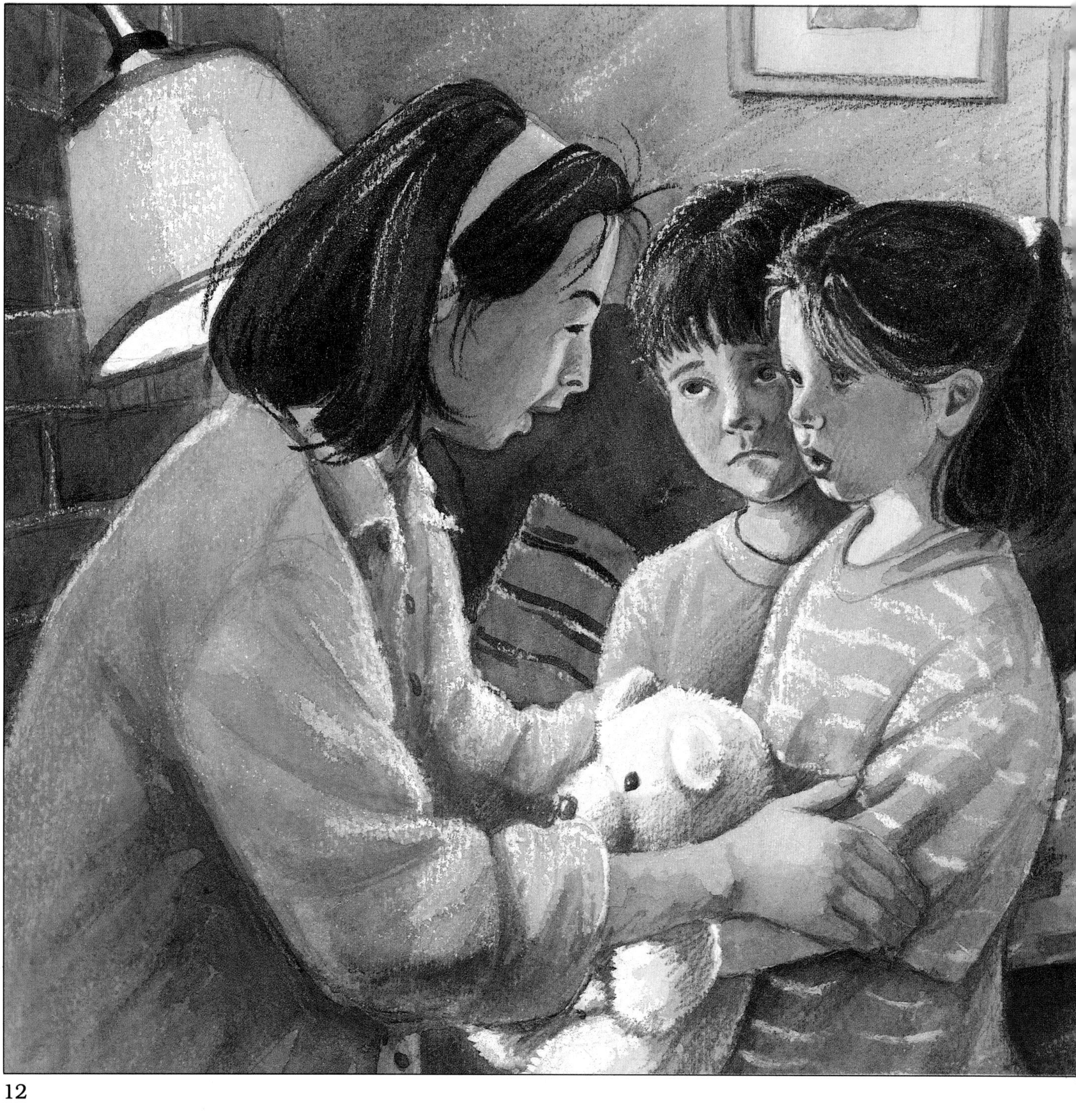

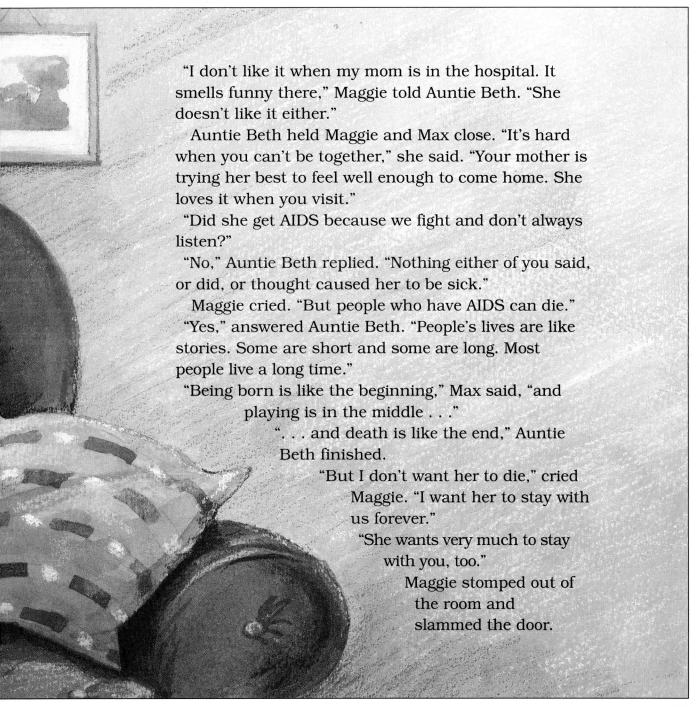

"I don't like it when my mom is in the hospital. It smells funny there," Maggie told Auntie Beth. "She doesn't like it either."

Auntie Beth held Maggie and Max close. "It's hard when you can't be together," she said. "Your mother is trying her best to feel well enough to come home. She loves it when you visit."

"Did she get AIDS because we fight and don't always listen?"

"No," Auntie Beth replied. "Nothing either of you said, or did, or thought caused her to be sick."

Maggie cried. "But people who have AIDS can die."

"Yes," answered Auntie Beth. "People's lives are like stories. Some are short and some are long. Most people live a long time."

"Being born is like the beginning," Max said, "and playing is in the middle . . ."

". . . and death is like the end," Auntie Beth finished.

"But I don't want her to die," cried Maggie. "I want her to stay with us forever."

"She wants very much to stay with you, too."

Maggie stomped out of the room and slammed the door.

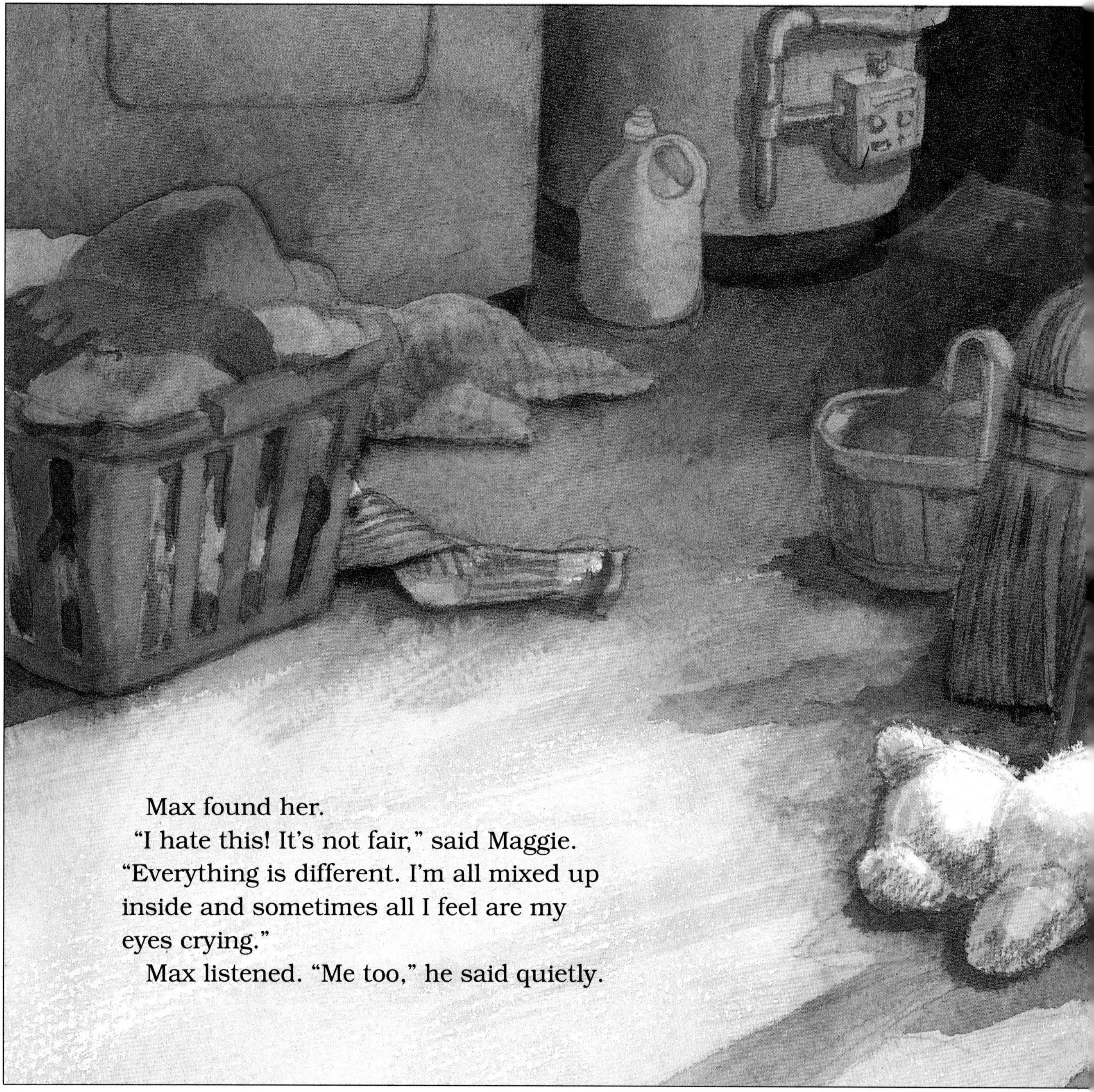

Max found her.
"I hate this! It's not fair," said Maggie. "Everything is different. I'm all mixed up inside and sometimes all I feel are my eyes crying."

Max listened. "Me too," he said quietly.

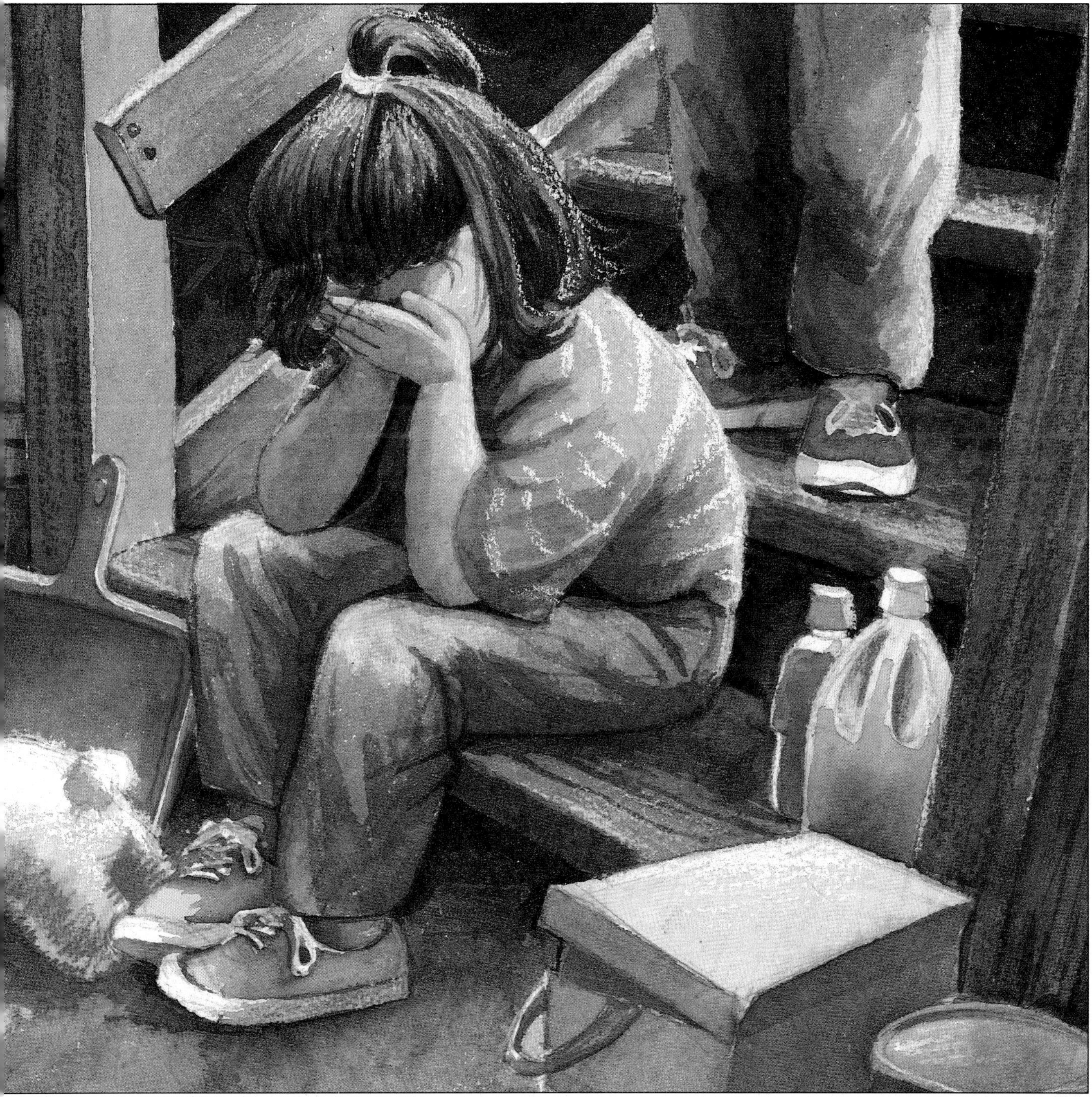

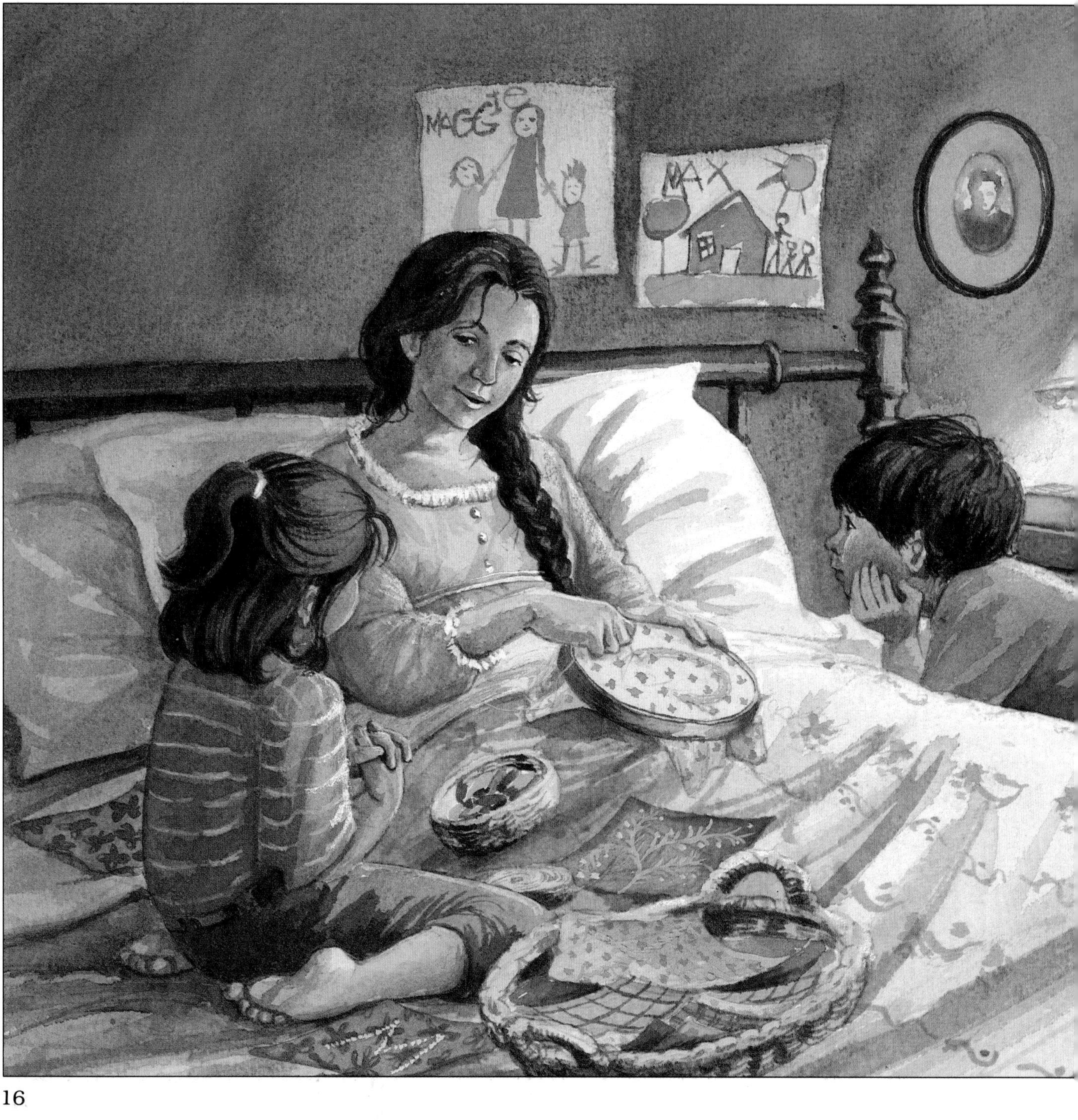
MAGGie
MAX

When Mother felt better she came home from the hospital. Max and Maggie set the table and brought her medicine. It was a very good day.

They talked late that night as Mother worked on the quilts she was making for them.

Maggie said, "It makes me so mad when people say stupid things about AIDS. What do they know?"

"Not as much as you," Mother told her. "You know you won't get AIDS by being with me, but the other children don't. You can help them understand about HIV infection."

"I'm glad you helped us understand," Max pointed out. "We don't have HIV infection, so we won't get AIDS."

When it was time for bed Max and Maggie sang her their song:

In the sky, a twinkling light,
Good night, star bright.
Soon will come the morning light,
Good night, sleep tight.

They whispered, "Dream a sweet dream tonight."

"I'll love you forever," Mother said.

"Me, too," added Max.

"Me, three," giggled Maggie.

Mother got sick more often. The doctor introduced Max and Maggie to someone new. His name was Martin and he helped them talk about their feelings.

"Mom has more bad days now," Max told Martin, while he drew a picture of what the bad days looked like. "I get angry easy," he admitted.

"She has some good days, too," added Maggie. "We help Auntie Beth and Uncle Dan take care of her."

"Come and talk with me any time you want," Martin always told them.

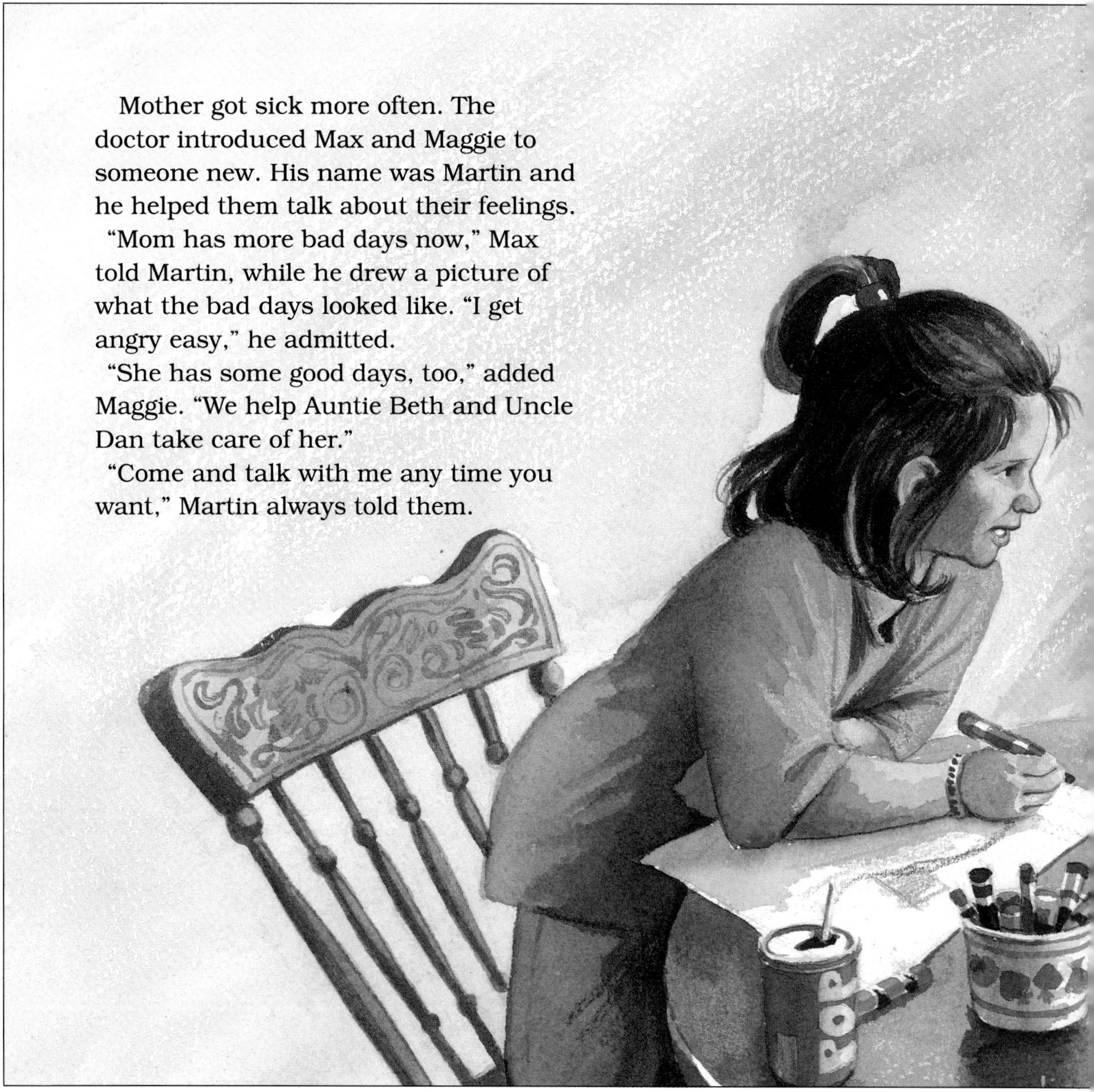
POP

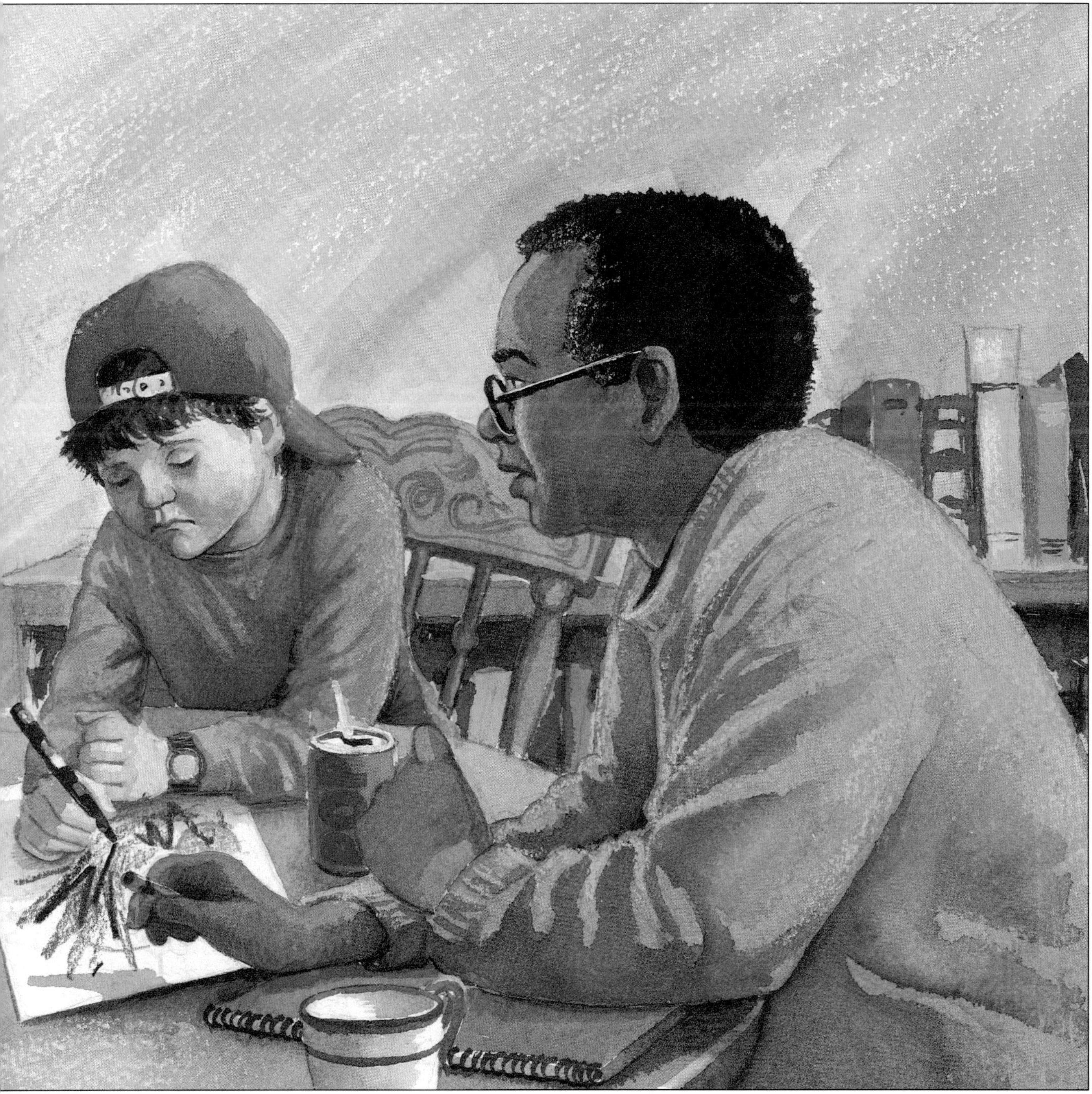

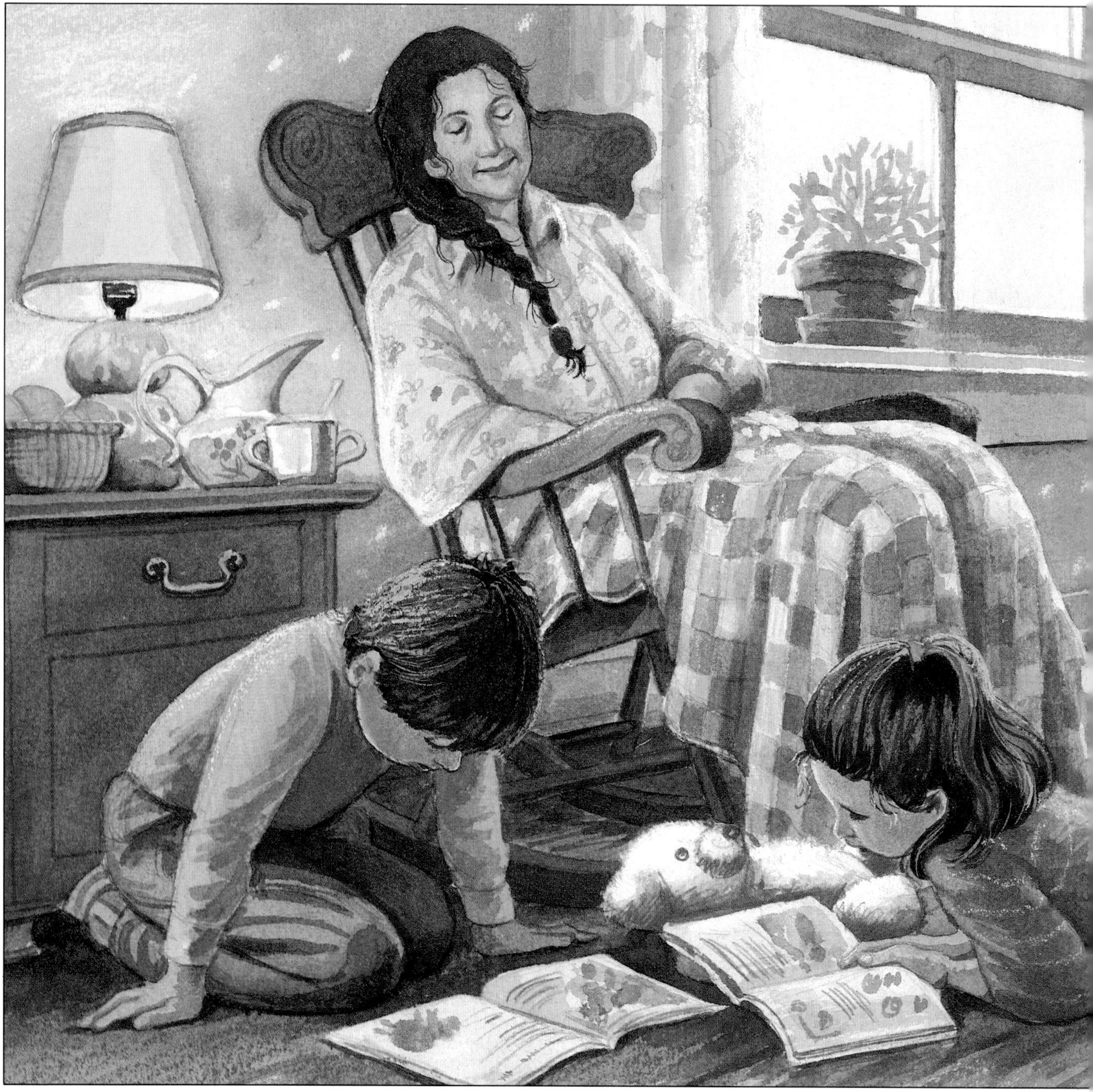

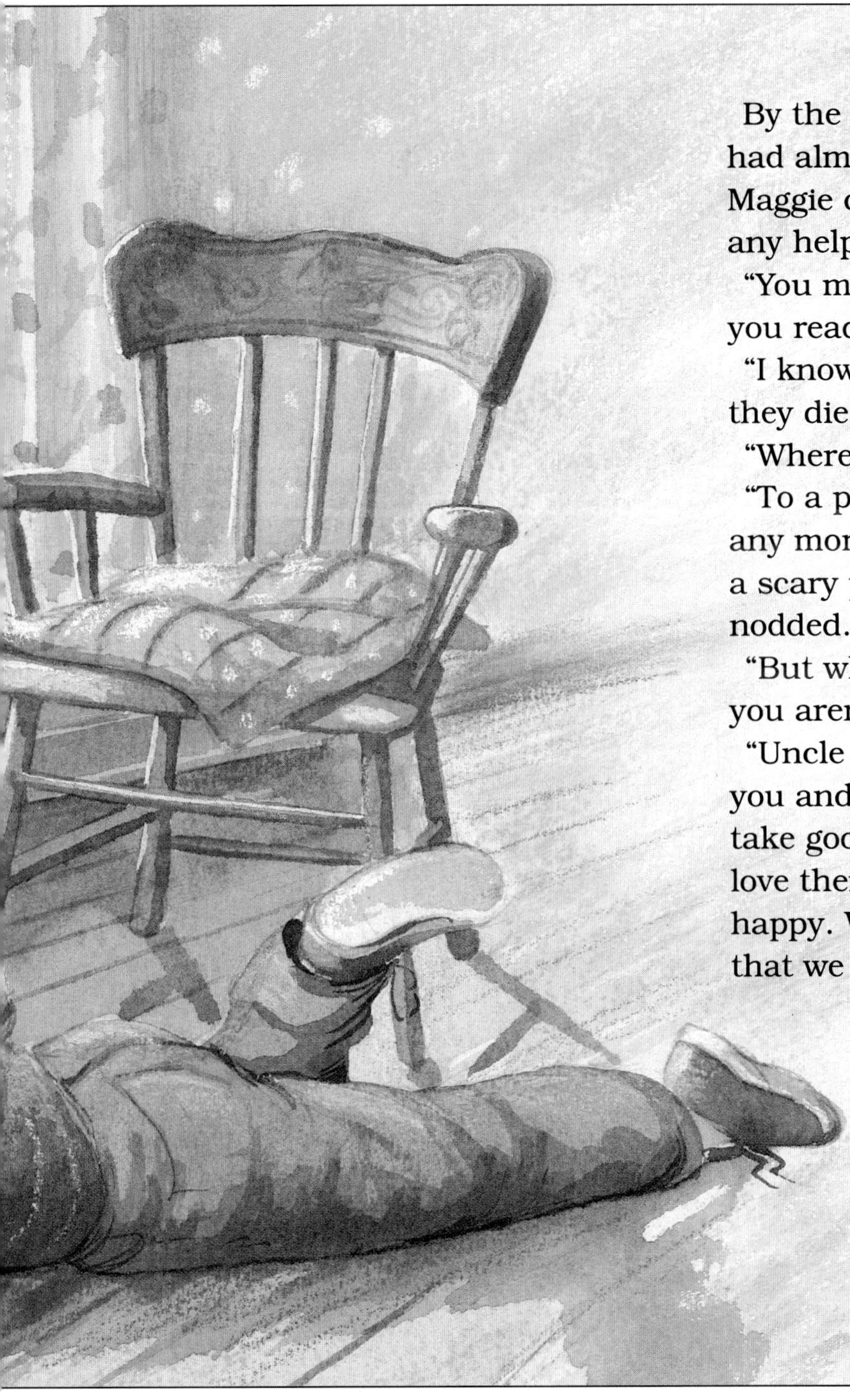

By the time the twins' big teeth had almost grown in, Max and Maggie could read with hardly any help.

"You make my heart sing when you read to me," said Mother.

"I know where people go when they die," Maggie announced.

"Where?" asked Mother.

"To a place where they don't hurt any more," she answered. "It's not a scary place." Mother smiled and nodded.

"But who will take care of us if you aren't here?" asked Max sadly.

"Uncle Dan and Auntie Beth love you and *promised* me they will take good care of you. I know you love them and that makes me happy. What's important now, is that we enjoy each other."

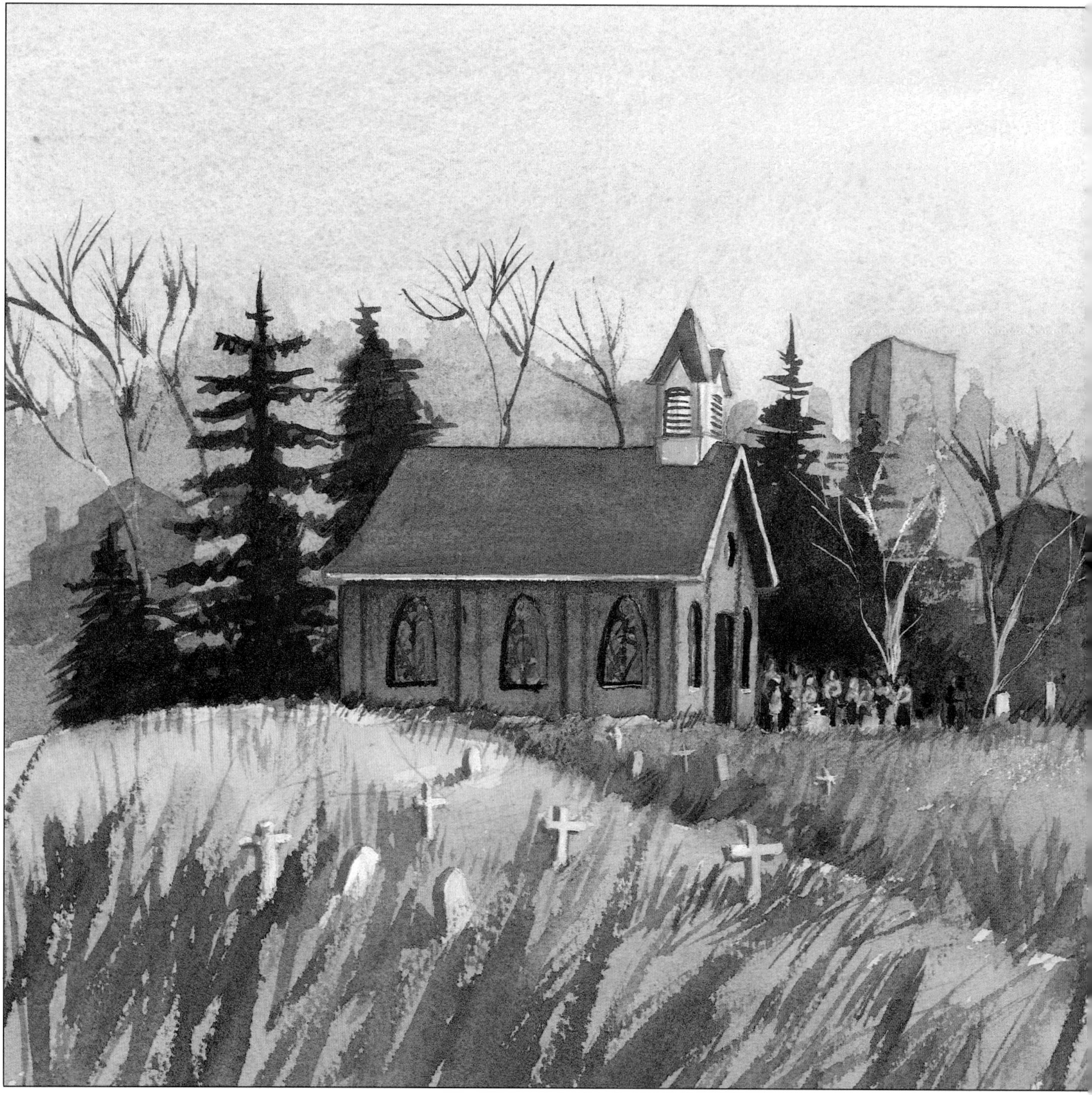

When Mother died, many people cried. A few days later, Max and Maggie went to her funeral with Auntie Beth and Uncle Dan. Mother's friends were there. They all came to say goodbye. It was a very, very sad time.

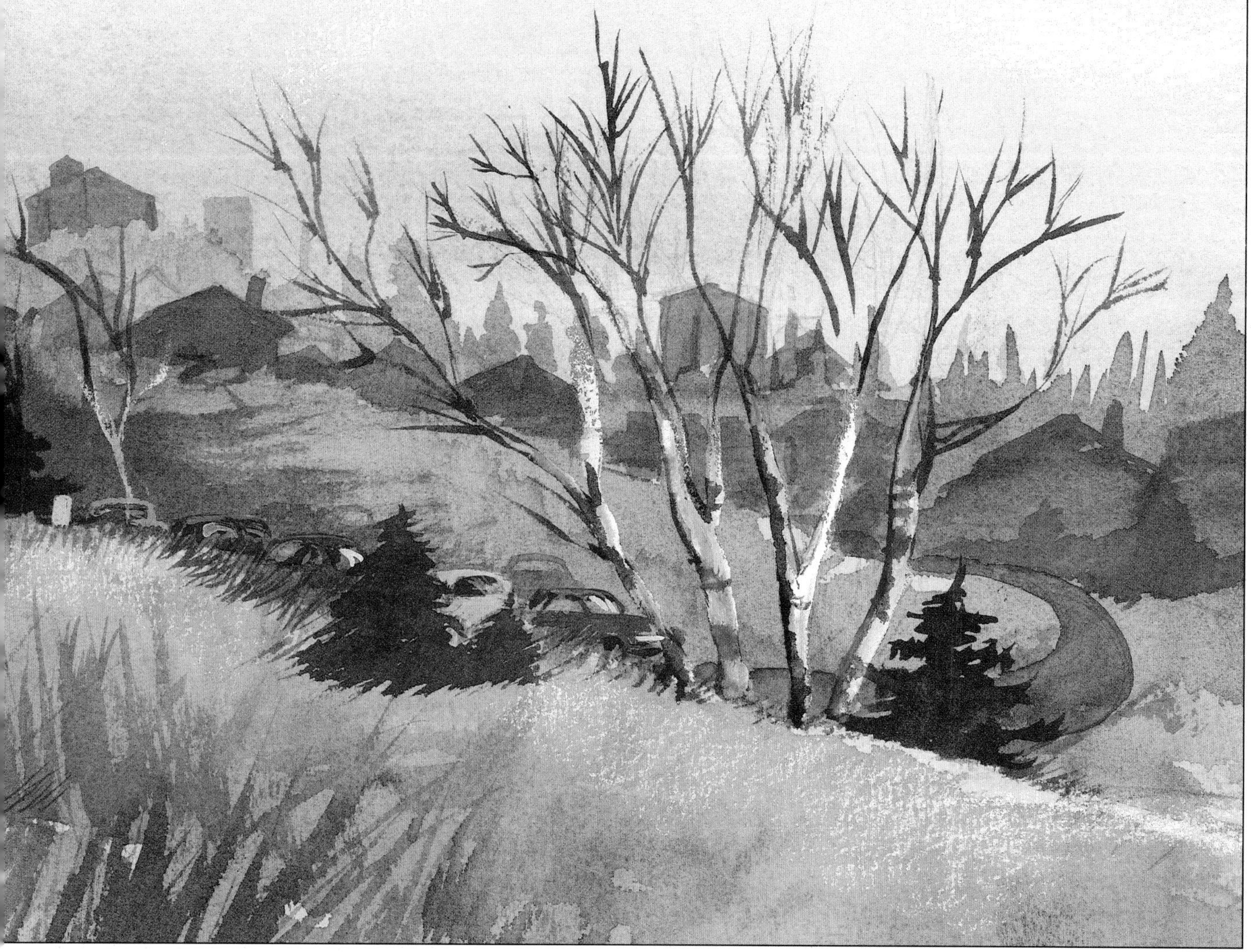

"When I try to sleep, tears roll into my ears," said Maggie.

"Mine do, too," answered Max. "Sometimes I think Mom will be there when I come home from school. When she isn't, I'm sad and then my head hurts. Martin says it will get better. He says even if we can't see Mom, we can still love her."

"Last night I saw Mom in my dreams, but sometimes when I'm awake, I can't remember her face," Maggie said.

Over the weeks and months that followed, Max and Maggie looked at pictures and told stories of when Mother was alive.

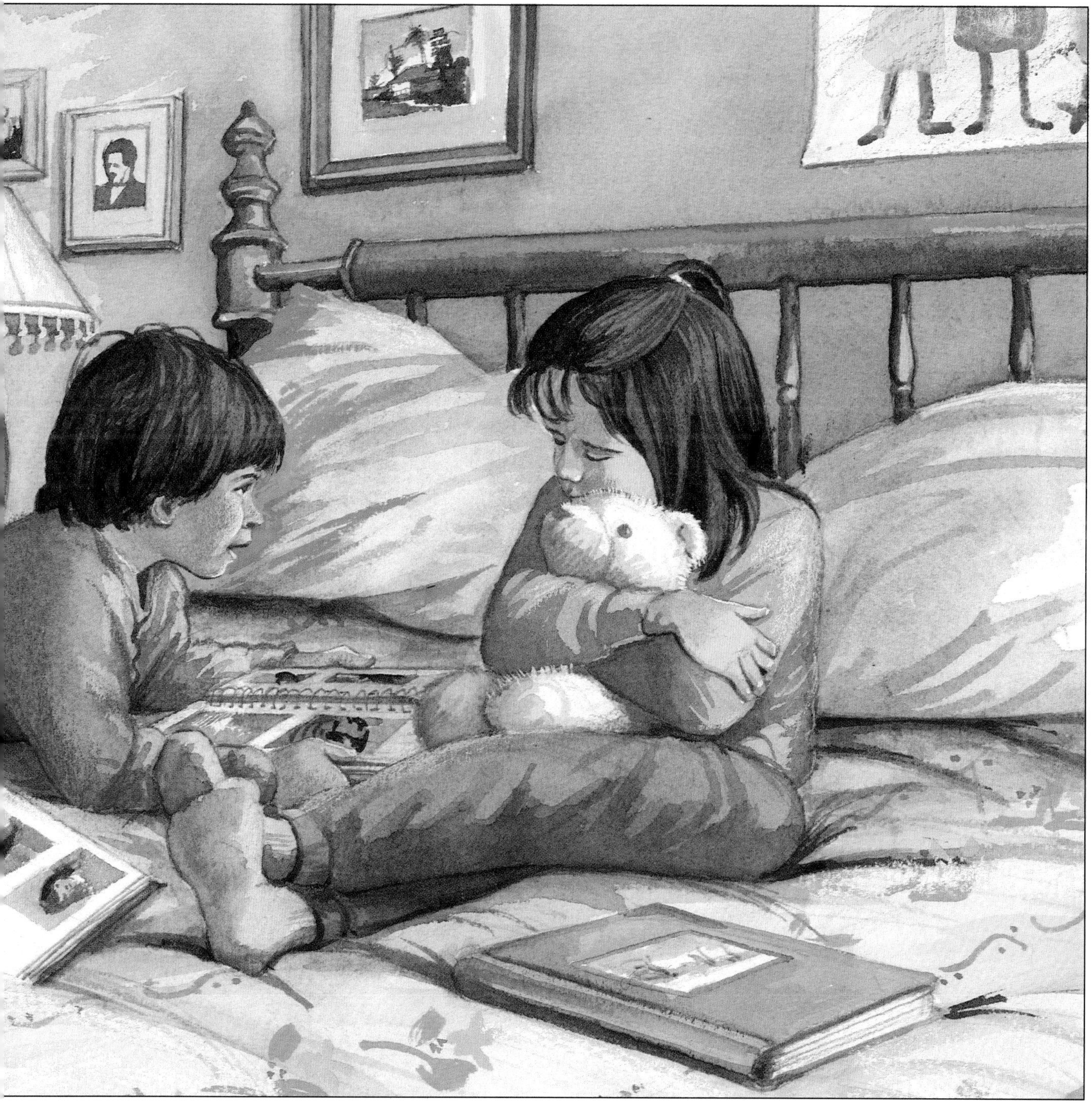

"Time to come in," Uncle Dan called to Max and Maggie. "It's getting dark."

As Max chased Maggie through the door, he tagged her and shouted, "I finally got you!"

"You did not!" Maggie shouted back. "I was already home free."

"Then I'll get you tomorrow."

"We'll see," taunted Maggie.

"Time for bed," Uncle Dan said.

The twins wrapped themselves in the quilts Mother had made and took turns singing to each other:

In the sky, a twinkling light,
Good night, star bright.
Soon will come the morning light,
Good night, sleep tight.

"Dream a sweet dream tonight," they whispered.

It was still a wonderful way to fall asleep.

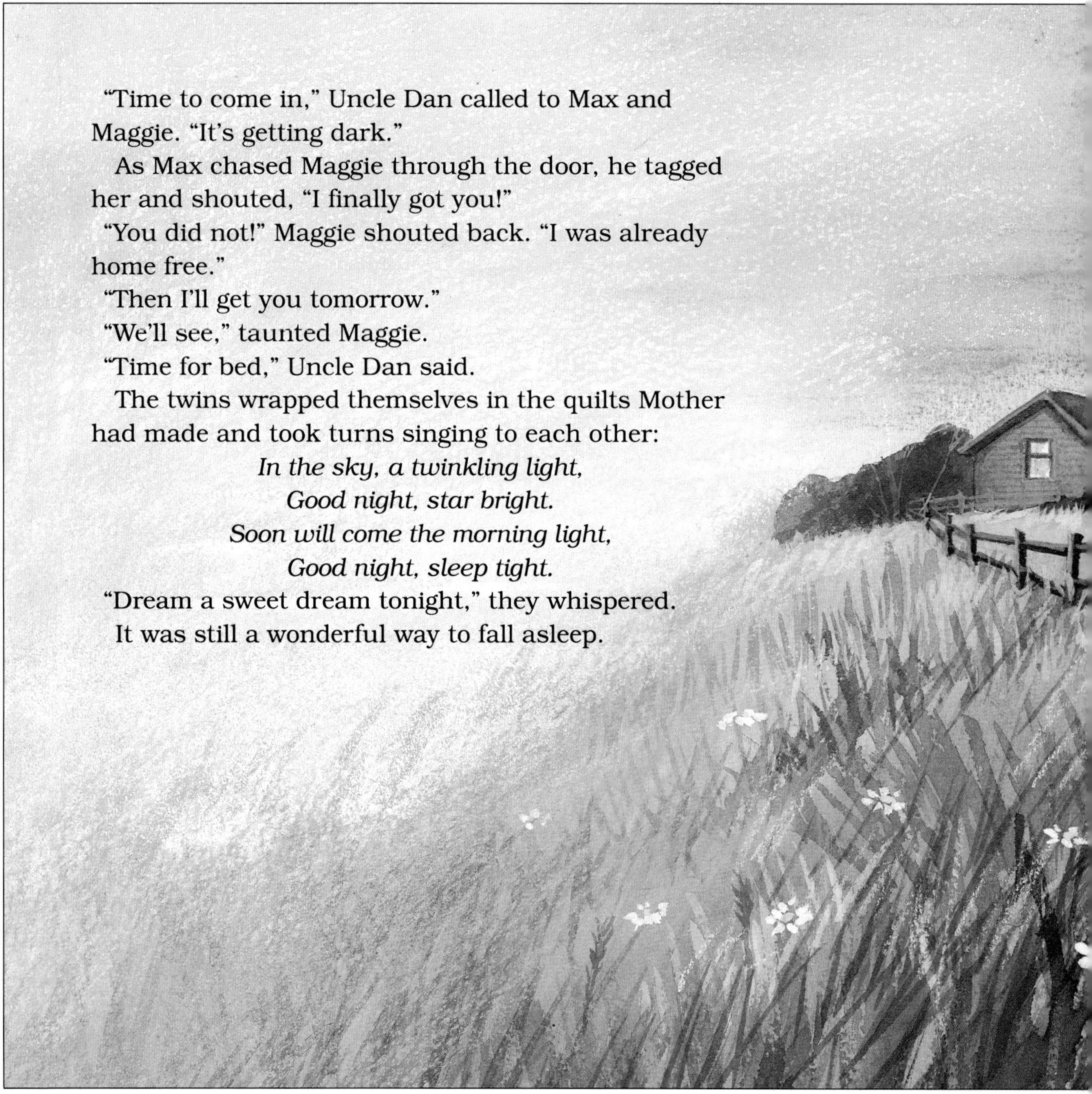

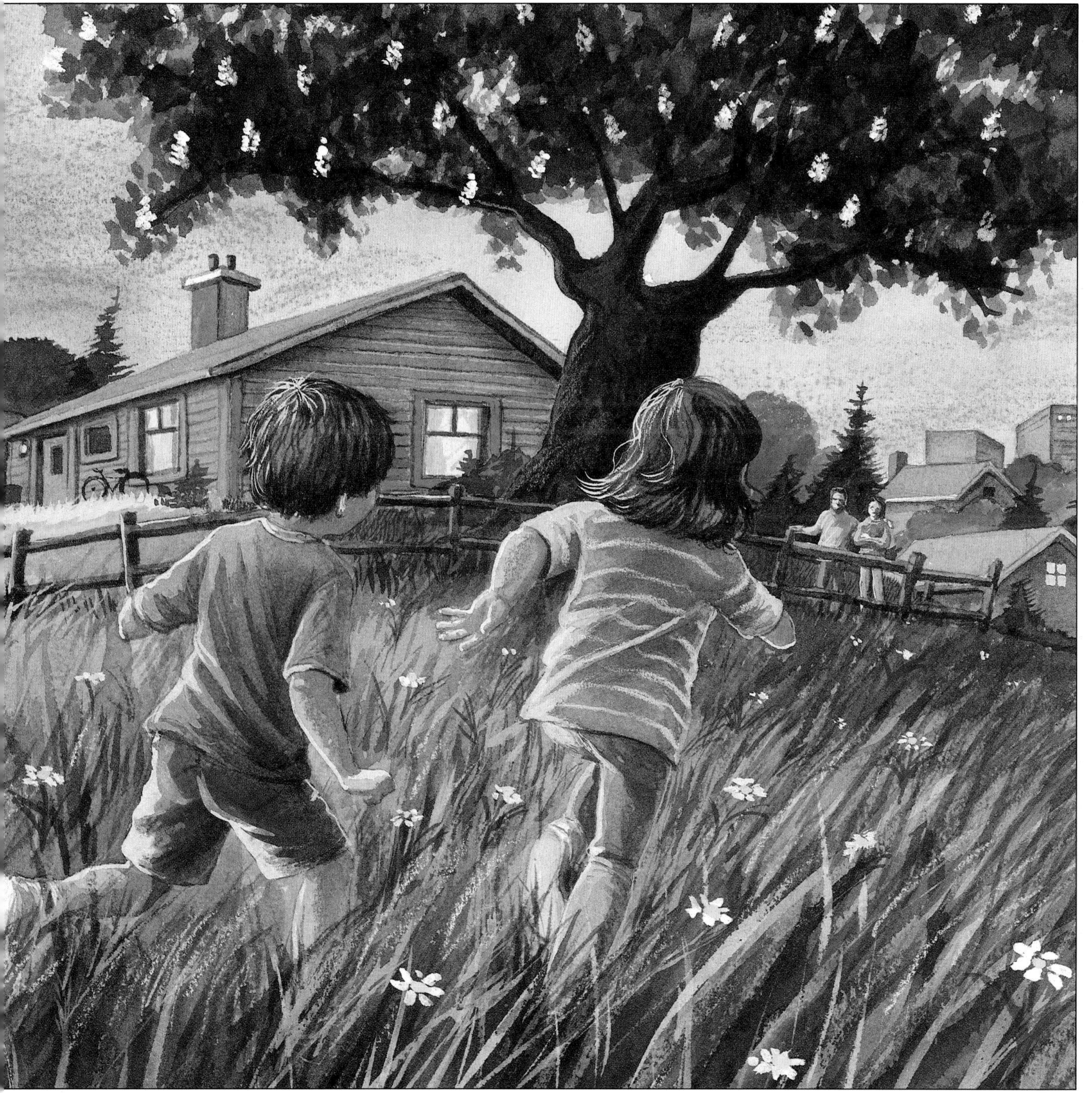

Acts of kindness are more helpful than

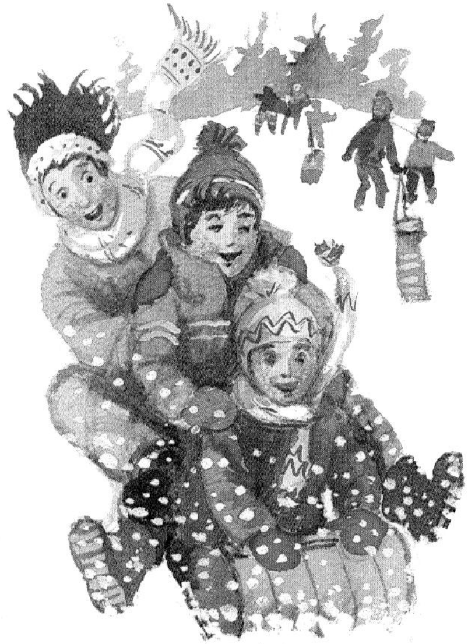

Playing together

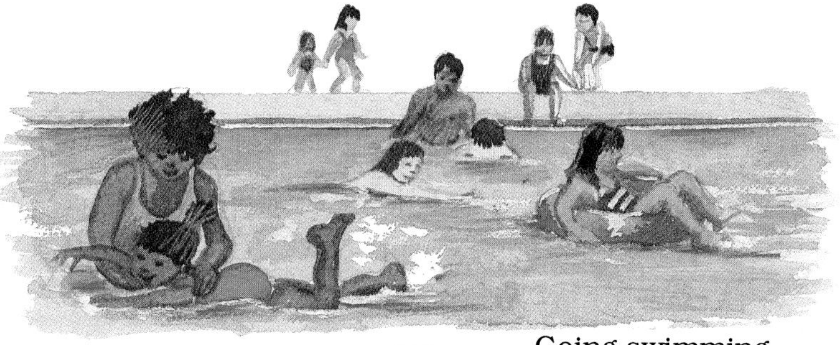

Going swimming

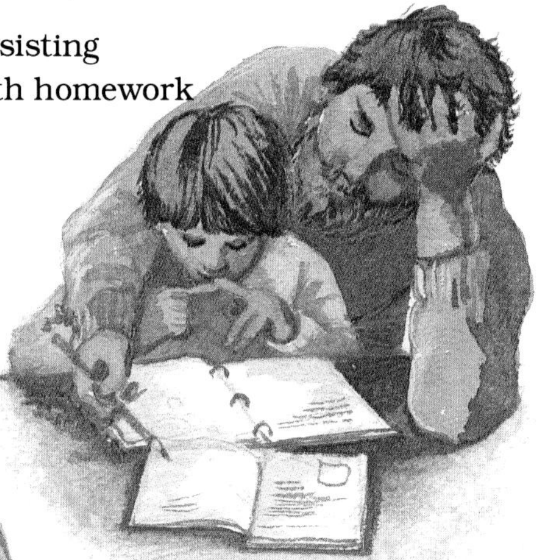

Assisting with homework

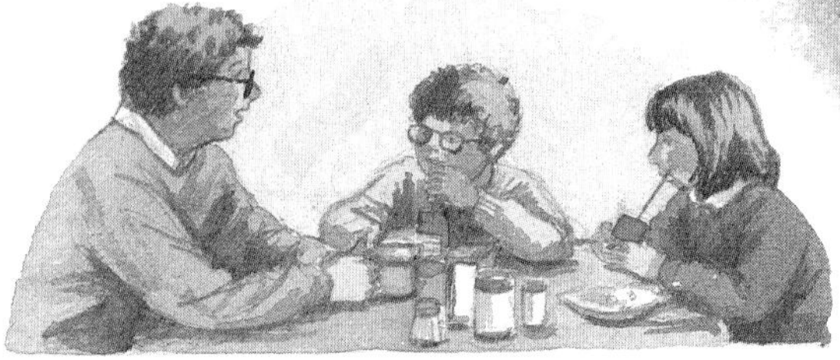

Sharing a meal

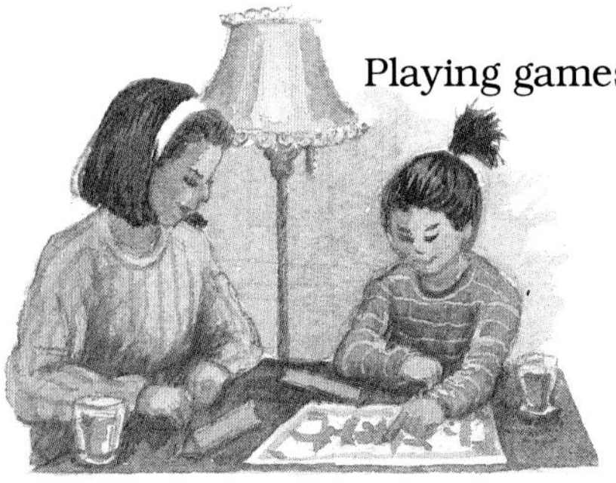

Playing games

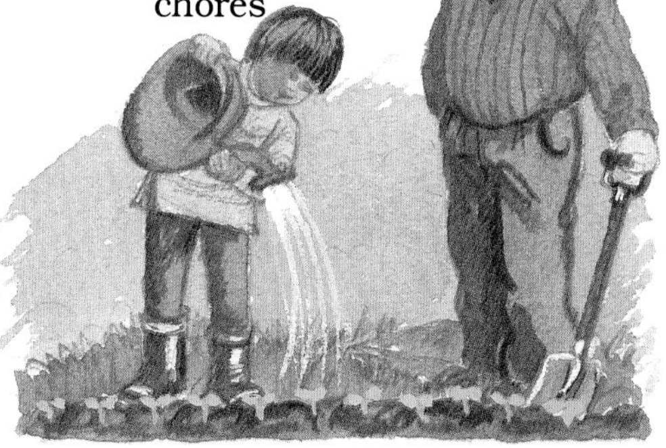

Working together and sharing chores

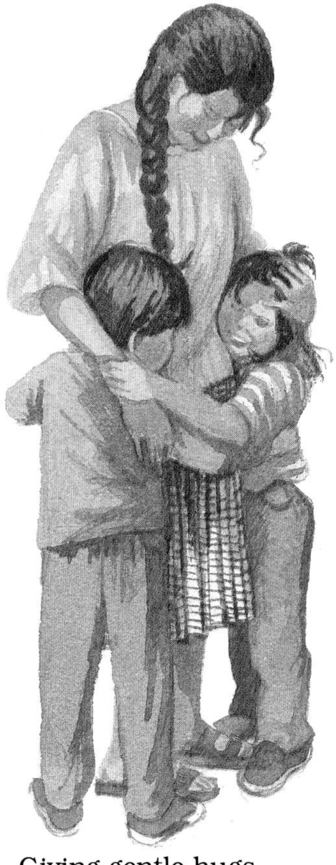

Giving gentle hugs and sharing tears

sympathetic words. You can help by:

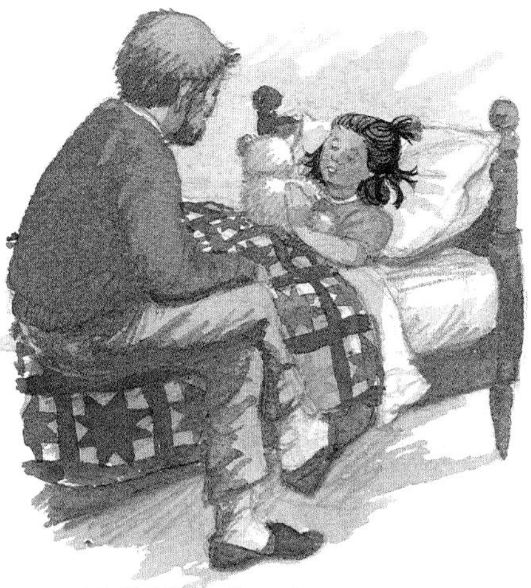

Talking about a possession that holds special meaning

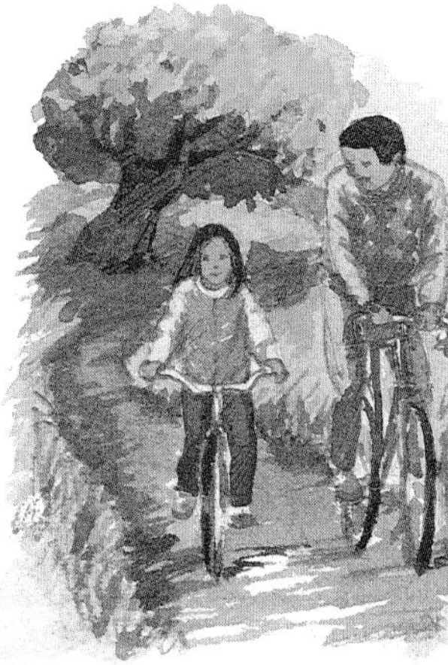

Riding bikes

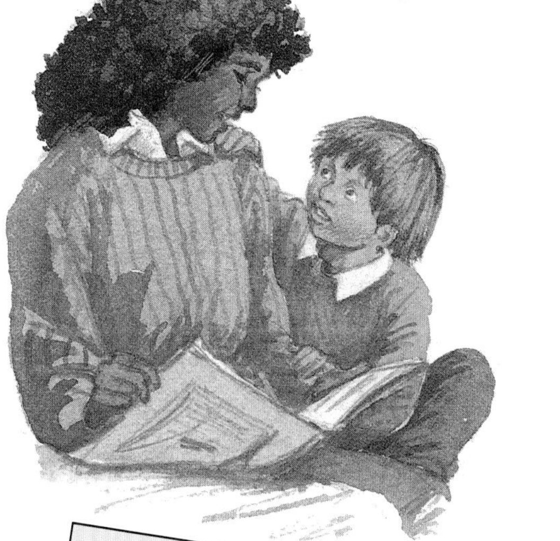

Listening attentively or sharing silence

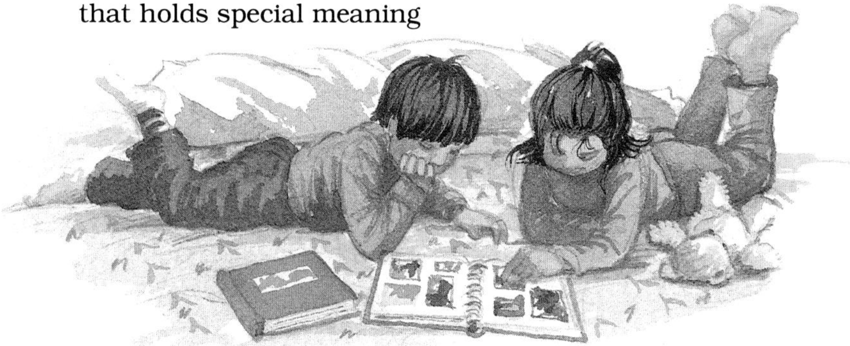

Looking at photos

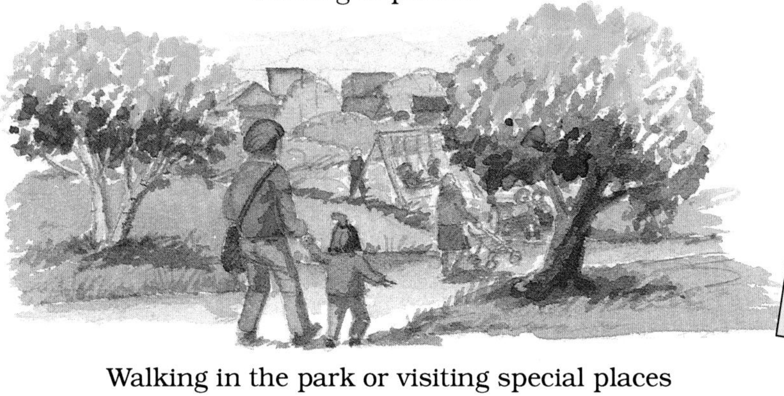

Walking in the park or visiting special places

It takes time to develop a self identity that no longer includes the person who died. It is extremely difficult for children to accept that once people have died, they are never coming back. Use words such as *dead* or *died.* It is helpful to say *I don't know for certain,* I am not sure, Many people think . . .

Phrases to avoid:

- went away on a long trip
- passed away, went to sleep
- be strong, cheer up
- you're young, you'll get over it
- big boys/girls don't cry
- the good die young
- you should be over it by now
- no sense dwelling in the past

Information For Students, Parents, Teachers and Caregivers About Death, Grief and Support

Introduction

Two things in life are certain. We are born and we will die.
Karen, Age 9

This section is written to increase awareness of how children understand death and dying. It provides practical child-centred information for those who 'walk with' grieving children.

Grief occurs when a person experiences a significant life loss. It is a natural response to life-changing events. Few people experience grief in orderly stages. The grieving or healing journey is exhausting intellectual, emotional, and spiritual work. It takes patience and courage. People travel at their own pace. It may take years.

With loss a person experiences shock, disbelief, anger, guilt, confusion, relief, fear, panic, loneliness, sadness, and powerlessness. Numbness is often the first response. Sometimes the body hurts as a result of such intense feelings of loss.

There is no right or wrong way to grieve.

With accurate information, patience, support, reassurance and time, children can be strong emotionally in spite of, and even because of their loss.

How children understand death and dying

Age, psychological development, emotional maturity, individual coping abilities, family environment, and culture affect a child's understanding of death.

Ages 3 to 5

Children have a 'here and now' concept of life and death. Younger children realize that being dead is different from being alive, and that death happens to others. By age 5, they *begin* to accept that death

comes to all living things, and is final and inevitable.

Ages 5 to 9

Children add details to this framework as their experience and knowledge increase.

Ages 9 to 12

Most children begin to view death in more abstract adult terms.

Common misperceptions

Infants and toddlers are too young to grieve.

Children are never too young to feel the loss of a primary relationship. Separation and loss are as much a part of life as attachment and belonging.

Children overcome loss more easily than adults.

Like grownups, children do not overcome loss. They live with it and work to adjust themselves to it. Grieving children are often abandoned shortly after the event because of this misperception.

Crying is a sign of weakness.

Crying is an important way of releasing emotional tension and asking for comfort.

Seeking professional help is an admission of inadequacy.

Asking for assistance during difficult times demonstrates understanding and courage.

It is better to keep the realities of death from children in order to protect them.

To make sense of their world, children need an understanding of both life and death.

They are more aware of death and dying than many adults realize.

How grief affects families

All families experience spoken and unspoken tensions that increase when a member dies. Physical and

emotional exhaustion complicates the grieving process. Children may feel neglected. Fewer problems develop when a child does not have to guess how others are feeling. When family interactions and roles inevitably change, a child should not be expected to become the 'man' or 'woman' of the house. Encourage children to be with their friends and involved in their usual activities.

How children grieve

Like adults, grieving children express their feelings in various ways. While they ask questions repeatedly, their verbal expressions are often limited by their vocabulary. Children will generally *show* how they feel. Some examples are:

- sleep disturbances
- headaches and stomach-aches
- an inability to concentrate
- age-inappropriate behaviours
- an increase in conflicts
- withdrawal from siblings, peers and parents.

Behaviours that require urgent professional attention include:

- persistent outbursts of intense anger
- persistent hyperactivity
- significant drops in school performance
- prolonged depression
- reliance on drugs or alcohol
- talk of suicide.

Grief attacks are waves of unexpected feelings that may be triggered by thoughts, sights, smells or sounds. They can occur months or years after the event. Anniversaries, birthdays, holidays or any day of personal significance are common triggers.

Special concerns

All families have unique circumstances that affect the grieving process. Sometimes existing problems such as HIV infection/AIDS or abuse complicate this difficult time. Professional advice can help.

HIV infection/AIDS

AIDS is a serious illness **complicated by a host of social issues** involving discrimination, confidentiality, public health policies, and child custody disputes. We need to be aware of and responsive to the special needs of children whose caregivers have died or are dying from AIDS. Children who are grieving will need special reassurance and honest answers to questions that arise.

Abuse

Abuse is the experience of unrelenting grief. Physically, emotionally, and sexually hurt children already suffer ongoing losses of dignity, trust and hope. Peer support groups and counselling are beneficial.

- Vulnerable children may feel intense ambivalence when an abusive parent or caregiver dies. Society *expects* them to mourn the loss. These children often experience relief. Others assume guilt or responsibility for the death because of intense feelings they may have had toward the abuser.
- Issues of safety arise when a non-offending parent or caregiver dies, leaving the child more at risk.
- If the child has never disclosed the abuse, the situation becomes more complex. Abusers burden children with responsibility, emotional threats and/or physical harm if they "ever tell." To tell the secret takes courage and trust. To hear it takes commitment and compassion. Trust is a core issue.

Ways to support a grieving child

Children need a **safe, secure, physical and emotional environment** in order to do the work of grieving. Notify the school or day care facility about the death. This will help teachers understand and respond effectively to any changes in the child's behaviour.

Reassurance is the foundation on which trust, imagination, and hope are built. Reassure the child again and again that:

- they or their caregiver are in no immediate danger of dying
- they will be taken care of
- most people live a long time
- their behaviour or thoughts were not responsible for the death
- feelings of anger are a common response.

Children require **open and honest explanations** from someone with whom they have a close relationship. Children, like adults, search for meaning in their lives. Grieving children learn early in life that people do not and cannot have complete control over themselves and their world. They often develop a deeper caring and compassion for others as a result of their experience. Answer what children want and need to know at a level they can understand. Children usually want to know:

- What happened?
  It is important that children be informed as soon as possible after the death. Gently explain what happened and try to encourage further conversation.
- What happens now?
  Tell the child what to expect next. Relatives and friends may come, there may be a funeral, there may be changes of routine the child will want to know about.
- Where do I fit in?
  Reassure children that although those around them may seem busy, preoccupied, and sad, they are still loved and important members of their family.
- Who will take care of me?
  Children instinctively know that they must rely on adults to nurture and provide for them. It is not insensitive or uncommon for a child to express self-concern when someone close dies. Let the children know as soon as possible who will meet their needs.

- Will I die too? Will I get AIDS?
  Explain that all living things eventually die, but that the child is in no immediate danger. If AIDS is the cause of death, explain that although AIDS is a very serious sickness, it is not like a cold or the flu. It is very difficult for a child to get.
- What happens when someone dies?
  Explain that people don't feel anything when they are dead. Their bodies no longer breathe, eat, run or play. Being dead is not like being asleep.

The funeral

For many families and friends, the funeral is an important occasion and a way to say goodbye. For children it can be a confusing time. Spiritual beliefs provide comfort to many people, but it is important to be aware that phrases such as *God took Mommy* or *Daddy's watching over you* can frighten or unsettle a child.

- Reassure the child again that dead bodies do not need to breathe and that the person feels no pain.
- Let them know what to expect and give them permission to attend *if they wish.*
- Allow them to choose the level of involvement they feel comfortable with. They may wish to draw a picture or act out a remembrance in song or story.
- Admit that adults do not have all the answers.
- Allow children to voice their own spiritual beliefs.

Grief support groups

Peer support groups help provide children with positive role models and the reassurance that:

- they are not alone
- their thoughts, feelings, and behaviours are normal and common
- they are not 'crazy'
- they can share stories and hear others speak of things they may be afraid to admit.

Resources

Check the phone book for local hospitals, hospices, AIDS organizations, community information listings, social service agencies, book stores, libraries, churches, and funeral homes. They are a good source of information. Your child's own doctor or school social worker can help guide you towards appropriate resources.

Suggested reading

Books for young children:

Where the Wild Things Are, by Maurice Sendak, Scholastic, New York, NY, ISBN 0-590-04513-X. A picture book that addresses the acting out of a small child and the ongoing love and support of a caring adult.

The Ten Good Things About Barney, by Judith Viorst, Aladdin Books, ISBN 0-689-71203-0. A small child mourns for his beloved cat, and with the help of his family, finds comfort in listing the good things about his pet.

The Saddest Time, by Nora Simon, Albert Whitman and Company, Niles, Ill, ISBN 0-8075-7203-9. An exceptionally sensitive and informative book portraying death and dying in three illustrated short stories.

Some of the Pieces, by Melissa Madenski, Little Brown and Company, ISBN 0-316-54324-1. The poignant story of how a family rebuilds itself after a great loss. A year after Dylan's father dies, Dylan, his mother, and sister share feelings and memories of him. Illustrated.

About Dying: An Open Family Book For Parents and Children Together, by Sara Bonnett Stein, Thomas Allen & Son, Canada, ISBN 0-8027-7223-4. This sensitive portrayal of the deaths of a bird and a grandfather is designed to provide a shared experience between adult and child. Illustrated with photographs.

Lifetimes, by Bryan Mellonie and Robert Ingpen, Bantam, ISBN 0-553-344. Tells about beginnings and endings and about living in between. With the help of large illustrations, it talks about plants, animals, and people and explains that all living things have their own special lifetimes. For parents and young children.

Come Sit by Me, by Margaret Merrifield, Women's Press, Toronto, Ontario, ISBN 0-88961-141-6. An information/picture book that addresses HIV/AIDS, compassion and tolerance. Includes an educational and resource section for children and caregivers.

Tiger Flowers, by Patricia Quinlan, Lester Publishing, Toronto, Ontario, ISBN 1-895555-58-2. A beautiful picture book about Joel and his Uncle Michael who comes to stay at Joel's house because he is dying of AIDS.

Books for middle aged children:

Charlotte's Web, by E.B. White, Harper Collins, ISBN 0-06-440055-7. The children's classic about a spider who dies after saving the life of her friend Wilbur the pig.

Mama's Going to Buy You a Mockingbird, by Jean Little, Puffin Books, Toronto, Ontario, ISBN 0-14-031737-6. When Jeremy learns his father is dying of cancer, everything is changed. This is a sensitive portrayal of a young boy's feelings as he comes to grips with the news of his father's illness, the realization that he is not going to recover, and his death. In the aftermath of this event, Jeremy learns that his father has given him something lasting.

Losing Uncle Tim, by Mary Kate Jordan, Albert Whitman and Company, Niles, Ill, ISBN 0-8075-4756-5. A sensitive story about a boy's relationship with an uncle who dies of AIDS.

Bridge to Terabithia, by Katherine Paterson Crowell, Harper Trophy, ISBN 0-06-440184-7. The award-winning story about friendship and death.

Learning to Say Goodby When a Child's Parent Dies, by Eda LeShan, Avon Books, New York, NY, ISBN 0-380-40105-3. A frank and intimate discussion about issues surrounding the loss of a parent. Topics include: It Has Happened, Grieving, Recovering from Grief, Death Teaches us About Life. An excellent and concise support for children to read by themselves or with an adult. A list of further resources is included. Some black and white line drawings accompany the text.

How it Feels When a Parent Dies, by Jill Krementz, Alfred A. Knopf, New York, NY, ISBN 0-394-75854-4. A collection of reflections on what it's like to lose a parent, by children ages 7 to 16. Personal viewpoints describe individual circumstances and feelings.

Accompanied by black and white photographs.

"Does AIDS Hurt?" Educating Your Child About AIDS, by Marcia Quackenbush and Sylvia Villarreal, Network Publications, Santa Cruz, CA, ISBN 0-941816-52-4. Suggestions for parents, teachers and other care providers of children to age 10.

Books for adults and teens:

Grief: The Courageous Journey, by Gordon Lang and Sandi Caplan, Cor Age Books, London, Ontario, ISBN 0-9696-8800-8. A concise, practical workbook and information source for teens and adults experiencing loss.

Cowboys Don't Cry, by Marilyn Halvorson, Stoddart Gemini, Toronto, Ontario, ISBN 0-7736-7394-6. Shane's world is shattered when his mother dies in an accident. His father, a rodeo star, turns to alcohol for comfort, leaving Shane even more abandoned.

Tiger Eyes, by Judy Blume, Dell Paperback, New York, NY, ISBN 0-440-98469-6. When her father is killed in a random shooting, a young girl must learn to cope with his death and the effect it has on her family.

When Living Hurts, by Sol Gordon, Dell Paperback, New York, NY, ISBN 0-440-20389-9. A what-to-do book for teens or friends who care about them when they feel discouraged, sad, lonely, hopeless, angry, depressed, suicidal.

Helping Children Grieve When Someone They Love Dies, by Theresa Huntly, Ausberg Fortress, Minneapolis, MN, ISBN 0-8066-2549-X. A concise and practical guide.

Young People and Death, Edited by John D. Morgan, The Charles Press, Philadelphia, PA, ISBN 0-914783-49-1. An excellent resource for caregivers.

A Child Dies: A Portrait of Family Grief, by Joan Hagan Arnold and Penelope Buschman Gemma, The Charles Press, Philadelphia, PA, ISBN 0-914783-72-6. Highly recommended. Interspersed with touching poems and stunning art.

AIDS-Proofing Your Kids: A Step by Step Guide, by Acker, Goldwater, and Dyson, Silvio Mattacchione and Company, Pickering, Ontario, ISBN 1-895270-09-X. Effective techniques to help solve complex problems.